DEADLY NEW YEAR

A RIGHT ROYAL COZY INVESTIGATION MYSTERY

HELEN GOLDEN

Drew Bradley Press

ALSO BY HELEN GOLDEN

A Right Royal Cozy Investigation Series

Tick, Tock, Mystery Clock (Novelette)

Spruced Up For Murder

For Richer, For Deader

Not Mushroom For Death

An Early Death (Prequel)

Deadly New Year (Novelette)

A Dead Herring

I Spy With My Little Die

A Cocktail to Die For

Dying To Bake

This is a work of fiction. Names, characters, places, and incidents are the product of the author's imagination, or she has used them fictitiously. Any resemblance to actual persons, living or dead, events, or locales is entirely coincidental.

ISBN (P) 978-1-915747-20-4

Edited by Marina Grout at Writing Evolution

Published by Drew Bradley Press

Cover design by Helen Drew-Bradley

First edition January 2023

NOTE FROM THE AUTHOR

I am a British author and this book has been written using British English. So if you are from somewhere other than the UK, you may find some words spelt differently to how you would spell them. In most cases this is British English, not a spelling mistake. We also have different punctuation rules in the UK.

However if you find any other errors I would be grateful if you would please contact me helen@helengoldenauthor.co.uk and let me know so I can correct them. Thank you.

For your reference I have included a list of characters in the order they appear and you can find this at the back of the book.

In terms of the timeline within the *A Right Royal Cozy Investigation* series, *Deadly New Year* takes place in between *Not Mushroom For Death* and *A Dead Herring.*

1

8:45 PM, THURSDAY 31 DECEMBER

Sophie Crammond stopped and scanned the room. *Where is he?* Her frantic search didn't reveal the stocky policeman from Fenshire CID. Was she going mad? She *had* seen him with Lady Beatrice and Perry Juke earlier, hadn't she? Now she doubted herself. Men in dinner jackets all looked the same to her. It was no good. He wasn't here in the Red Ballroom. *I'll have to try the Salon. Maybe he's in the temporary bar set up just off the Painted Hall.* She scurried back out of the ballroom and made her way across the black-and-white tiled floor of the impressively huge hallway. Just as she got halfway across, something caught her eye and she turned her head. She couldn't mistake that slim frame encased in a beautiful full-length gold gown. *Lady Beatrice!* The king's niece disappeared behind the magnificent staircase. *She'll do just as well!*

Immediately changing direction, the head housekeeper rushed towards the staircase, weaving and bobbing between party guests. She hurled herself around the bottom of the stairs and just saw Lady Beatrice's gold-clad foot disappearing into the corridor leading towards the back stairs. "Lady Beatrice!" she cried as she stopped to get her breath.

"Mrs C?" A head piled high with red hair appeared from around the wall.

"My lady, thank goodness I've found someone." Mrs Crammond moved towards the woman, who was now in full view, her forehead creased by a frown.

"Mrs C. What's up?" Perry Juke appeared from around the corner and walked beside Lady Beatrice as they approached.

Mrs Crammond suppressed a sigh. They both looked so glamorous and happy. And now she was going to spoil their evening. *I'm so sorry...*

"Mrs C, what's wrong?" Lady Beatrice asked as they stood in front of each other, her voice full of concern, her brown eyes wide.

"Lady Beatrice, Perry, I'm sorry, but there has been an accident, and..." She took a deep breath. "Jasmine Curson is dead."

2

TWO DAYS EARLIER, TUESDAY 29 DECEMBER

The Society Page online article:

Lady Beatrice to Host the Annual Staff Ball at Francis Court in Fenshire

Lady Beatrice (36), the Countess of Rossex, will host the annual Francis Court staff ball this year on New Year's Eve. The ball, a tradition at Francis Court, is held each year to say thank you to the two hundred staff and their partners who work at the family's sixteenth-century stately home and its 25,000-acre estate on the North Fenshire coast in Francis-next-the-Sea.

Francis Court is the seat of Lady Beatrice's father Charles Astley, the Duke of Arnwall (63), and his wife Her Royal Highness Princess Helen (63), the sister of King James. The ball will take place in the Red Ballroom, one of the staterooms in the east wing of Francis Court, and is a highly anticipated event. Posh and Fabulous, the much sought after Fenshire-based event's company owned by high-

society sisters, Jasmine Curson (32) and Holly Curson (30), are providing the party planning and catering for the ball.

3

MORNING, TUESDAY 29 DECEMBER

"But what happens if it's a disaster, Ma?" Lady Beatrice, the Countess of Rossex, wore a path into the plush carpet in her mother's dressing room as she paced back and forth, twisting the rings on her right hand. On a nearby chaise lounge, sat her white West Highland terrier Daisy, her head following her mistress as she moved in front of her.

"It won't be, darling. We've been hosting the staff ball here for twenty years. and it's always been a huge success," HRH Princess Helen replied as she hauled out a beautiful deep-red ballgown from her floor-to-ceiling built-in wardrobe and carefully carried it to a temporary hanging rail over by the door.

Pressure! "Yes, but that's because you or Sarah hosted it in the past. I've never done anything like this before." Her palms damp, Lady Beatrice wiped them down her skinny black jeans. Why on earth had she agreed to take on hosting duties from her mother and sister at the annual staff ball this year? It wasn't like she didn't have enough on her plate already with preparing to go to Scotland to manage the refurbishment project at Drew Castle, the king's private estate in the Highlands, that started in the new year. And there was her fourteen-year-old son Sam. He was due home from his paternal grandparents later today, and she really wanted to spend some quality time with him, feeling like she'd barely seen him this holiday. He'd be going back to boarding school next week, the day before she journeyed up to Scotland, and it would be weeks before she'd be able to get from there to Wilton College to see him.

"Darling?" Her mother's voice dragged her from her thoughts. "I said, do you think it's too cliche to wear this to the formal New Year's Day lunch?" She held up a calf-length emerald-green dress with black roses on the flared skirt, her head to one side as she studied the tea dress. "Pa will be wearing his kilt, so do you think it will all be a bit too Irish?"

Lady Beatrice stopped pacing and, turning, smiled at her mother. "How can you be too Irish, Ma? You're going to be in Ireland, and they'll expect you to look the part. It's perfect."

Her mother nodded and placed the dress next to the red ballgown on the rail, then moved towards her, holding out her hands to her youngest daughter. "Beatrice, I know it feels a little overwhelming, but you'll be fine, I promise. I know Sarah and I are rather dropping you in at the deep end, but I have to go to Kilkirk House with your father. He's committed to keeping the estate running if he can make it financially sustainable, and that depends a lot on the goodwill of the locals. And it was so lovely for Sarah to get away. She and John work so hard. A week in the sun without the children is just what they need." She gave Lady Beatrice's hands a reassuring squeeze, then dropped them and walked back to her grand closet.

Of course. Her sister worked tirelessly to keep Francis Court running smoothly, and her brother-in-law's investment business in the city was thriving because of the long hours and hard work he put in. *They deserve a break.* She just wished it could be *after* the staff ball!

"And with the Curson sisters running the show and Mrs Crammond and Ellie Gunn on hand to muck in, the whole thing will practically run itself," her mother continued over her shoulder.

Lady Beatrice sighed. *I hope so!* She just wanted it to be the perfect evening for the staff as a tribute to how hard they had worked all year.

Leaving her parents' apartment on the second floor of Francis Court, Daisy trotting beside her, Lady Beatrice descended the large stone staircase that was the central feature of the Painted Hall at Francis Court. She was pleased to see preparations for the ball had already started, with tables and chairs stacked up by the underside of the staircase, next to boxes piled up with what looked like linens and shimmering gold wall hangings. A shiver of anticipation ran down her spine. *Please let this be a success.* She didn't want to let the staff down.

Reaching the bottom of the stairs, she spotted the head housekeeper Mrs Crammond disappearing into the Red Ballroom in the east wing and sped up to follow her. "Mrs C," she cried once she was within a decent distance of her.

The woman's short brown bob of thick hair flicked away from her face as she stopped and spun around. "Daisy." A smile spread over her round face, and she bent down to fuss over the white terrier, who had reached her ahead of her mistress. Lady Beatrice smiled to herself. She was used to everyone greeting her little dog first. The shorter woman rose, a smile still on her face. "Ah, Lady Beatrice. That's good timing. I was hoping to catch you this morning. Jasmine has a couple of changes she'd like to make to the decorations for the Salon and wants to run them by you. Do you have time now, my lady?"

Lady Beatrice looked at her watch. She and Perry Juke, her business partner, were due on a video call with a Scottish supplier in half an hour about the imminent Drew Castle project. "If it's fairly quick, Mrs C. I have a meeting in thirty minutes."

Mrs Crammond nodded and retrieved a mobile phone from her pocket. "I'll text her now and ask her to meet us there."

As Lady Beatrice waited, she scanned the Red Ballroom, noting that the Christmas decorations (put up especially for the three weeks in December when the house was open to the public, showing off how it would have looked during a Victorian Christmas) had been replaced with gold ones in line with the Hollywood-glamour theme they'd agreed on for the ball. It looked spectacular.

"She'll meet us there now," Mrs Crammond told her as she shuffled towards the door.

"Indeed." Lady Beatrice followed her out. "The ballroom looks stunning, Mrs C."

Sophie Crammond nodded as they made their way across the black-and-white tiled floor of the Painted Hall with Daisy trotting between them. "Yes, her team has been working very hard." There was something in the housekeeper's voice that caught Lady Beatrice's attention. She was about to ask her what was wrong but didn't get a chance as they entered the Salon, a reception room off the main hall where the bar was going to be set up. An attractive woman with long straight hair strutted across the room to meet them, her hands on her curvaceous hips as if she was a runway model.

"Mrs Crammond," the woman greeted the housekeeper, then, ignoring Daisy, who was sitting almost in front of her, her white tail wagging, turned to stare expectantly at Lady Beatrice.

"Hello, Jasmine." Mrs Crammond's voice had a slight edge to it. "I don't think you've met Lady Rossex, have you? Lady Rossex, this is Jasmine Curson from Posh and Fabulous."

As Lady Beatrice took Jasmine's hand and returned the woman's gaze, a pair of piercing blue eyes framed by enormous black eyelashes stared back. But while there was a broad smile plastered on Jasmine's smooth face, there was no warmth in her eyes. Lady Beatrice suppressed a shiver as the woman spoke.

"Lady Rossex, so good to finally meet you. It's normally your sister Lady Sarah who I liaise with for events."

Lady Beatrice bristled. Jasmine had made it sound like she was a poor substitute for her sister. She looked over at Sophie Crammond and could see from the look on the housekeeper's face that she wasn't the only one who wasn't signing up to be Jasmine's new best friend any time soon.

"We're really looking forward to Thursday night. It will be wonderful." She flicked her blonde tresses away from her face with one hand. "I've had a few ideas about this room that I'd like to run by you. To complement the gold theme, I'd like to add some feathers, my lady. White and gold ones. Big, brash, and beautiful."

Fifteen minutes later and feeling like she never wanted to see a picture of another feather again in her life, Lady Beatrice was glad when a text from Perry asking her where she was gave her an excuse to leave them to it. *I'm sure it will all look amazing,* she told herself as she and Daisy hurried to the Old Stable Block where their office was.

"So how's the ball prep going?" Perry tilted his blond head to one side as he took a sip of his coffee. The virtual meeting was over, and Lady Beatrice was glad for the chance to have a hot drink and take a breath.

She shifted in her chair so she could cross her legs and said, "It's coming together from what I can see. The events' people seem to have it all under control. That's why I was running late. I've just had a brief meeting with Jasmine Curson."

Perry wrinkled his nose. "Oh, the fabulous Jas Curson. What do you think of her?"

She hesitated. Something about the way Perry had said 'fabulous' in a faintly snarky way made her think he wasn't a fan either. "I didn't really take to her. She seemed too cool for school, *and* she ignored Daisy." She looked over at her little white terrier snoozing in her bed in the corner of the office. Anyone who didn't say hello to a dog was someone to be wary of in her mind.

"Yeah. She's a bit of an acquired taste." He put his hand up. "Although, to be fair, she's very good at her job. Wait until you see her on the night. She can schmooze guests like you wouldn't believe. She rolls out her boyfriend Leo Pack. He's a model. And they walk around like they own the place, saying just the right thing to make people feel welcome and special. It's a sight to see."

"Indeed. I've seen her around at some of the events here that Sarah's organised. I've just never met her before. But

Sarah talks highly of her and the team. She's striking, isn't she? What's her sister like? Holly, isn't it?"

"Holly's a few years younger and much quieter. She prefers to stay in the background and do the organising of the staff and food. She's very efficient."

Lady Beatrice nodded. "They sound like they complement each other well."

Perry shrugged. "I'm not sure they always see eye to eye, but it never shows when they're running an event." She raised an eyebrow. He continued, "I think Jas rather likes to have her own way. She recently took on a new chef, Aaron someone, who she pinched from a restaurant in Mayfair at great expense. Holly wasn't happy as Jas didn't consult her beforehand. She only knew about it when he turned up for his first event."

"That's very heavy-handed."

"Yes. Even Leo told Jas she owed Holly an apology, but she treats him like she's Father Christmas and he's her little elf, so she took no notice. It caused a bit of a fuss for a while. Although I'm sure they've got over it by now."

"Well, let's hope so. I need this party to go smoothly with no drama."

4

LATE AFTERNOON, THURSDAY 31 DECEMBER

"Well, I think that's all in order, Holly," Mrs Crammond said as she handed the costing sheet back to the dark-haired woman as they sat in her office. "And how's everything else going business wise? Are you busy?"

"Oh yes, Mrs Crammond."

She was well spoken. *No doubt because of the expensive school she and her sister went to,* Mrs Crammond thought.

Pushing her reading glasses up the bridge of her nose, Holly continued, "We seem to be inundated with requests to quote for events. Not that I'm complaining, of course." She smiled, although it didn't quite reach her eyes.

She looks tired. Maybe the gossip that Sophie Crammond had heard about Holly doing all the work while Jasmine swanned around, Leo in tow and taking all the glory, was true.

Holly Curson rose and tucked a stray wisp of hair behind her ear, then tried to push it up into the tight ponytail at the back of her head. She gave up and said, "Anyway, Mrs Crammond, if that's all, I really need to get on."

"Yes, of course," Sophie said as she stood. "The house is

looking amazing already, Holly. I'm sure it's going to be a great success and Lady Beatrice will be relieved. This is her first time hosting an event here, so we're all doing what we can to make sure it goes smoothly."

The woman nodded. "I understand, and we at Posh and Fabulous will support you every step of the way." She smiled, then turned and hurried out of the room.

Sophie Crammond sat down again and rested her chin on her hands. Something felt off with the event planners. A tension that she'd not seen before. She sighed. This was Lady Beatrice's first year as host, and she wanted it to be a huge success for her. *It's funny how this time last year I barely knew her. She was just Lady Sarah's slightly snooty younger sister, who was rarely seen around the place. But since I've got to know her over the last year, I've actually grown quite fond of her.*

———

"Are you excited, Mum?" Sam Wiltshire asked his mother, who was sitting at the dressing table in their apartment on the first floor in the west wing of Francis Court, trying to apply her lipstick. *Why am I shaking? It's just a party.* What happens if the staff don't enjoy it? *Get a grip, Bea. It will be fine.*

"Mum?"

"Sorry, darling. Yes, I am. But if I'm honest, I'm rather jealous that you and your cousin get to chill in your pyjamas watching films and playing games while I'm wearing these ridiculous heels and all trussed up in this dress. I will no doubt eat way too much cheese fondue and burst out of the sides! Can we do a swap? Will you go in my place, and I'll hang out with Robbie?"

Sam laughed. "No way!"

"All right, darling. You enjoy your evening, and I'll pop up and see you later."

As Sam ran out of the room, she turned back to the mirror. She nervously patted the back of her hair where it swept up into a mass of red curls piled on top of her head. She picked up the can of hairspray and sprayed a fine mist over her hair. *I hope that holds.* She grabbed her right hand with her left and steadied it, then picking up the nude lipstick, she took a deep breath and applied it.

She rose, and smoothing down the skirt of her dress, she walked towards the door just as Daisy appeared from the bedroom and joined her mistress.

"Come on, lazy bones, I need you with me for moral support." Daisy was a wonderful distraction. The staff were used to seeing her around Francis Court, and they would be delighted to see her tonight. She picked up her phone and, opening the door, watched her little white dog trot past her into the corridor.

An hour later, she was questioning her earlier decision to wear sky-high Louboutin heels. Her feet throbbed, and her toes were numb. "Perry, I think I'm going to have to change my shoes," she said to her elegant blond-haired companion, whose arm she was currently using to keep herself steady. "Do you think anyone will notice if we pop upstairs to my apartment? It won't take long. We can also check on the boys." She'd been too busy meeting and greeting guests to have had time to see if Sam and Robbie had eaten all the snacks she'd left them and gone into a sugar coma yet.

"Everyone's here now, and they're happily indulging on canapés. I don't think they'll miss us for a short while."

"Great," she said, steering him towards the sweeping staircase, Daisy following. "But just to be on the safe side, let's go up through the servants' stairs."

The three of them made their way around the back of the giant stone staircase. They just reached the start of the corridor that would lead them to the back stairs when a voice shouted, "Lady Beatrice!" She looked at Perry and sighed. "That sounds like Mrs C. We'd best see if she's okay."

They turned and retraced their steps. As they rounded the corner, a rather breathless Sophie Crammond greeted them. "My lady, thank goodness I've found someone," she said as she moved towards them.

"Mrs C. What's up?" Perry asked as they stopped in front of her.

A look of concern was already plastered across her flushed face.

Oh no, something is wrong. "Mrs C, what's wrong?" she asked quickly.

"Lady Beatrice, Perry, I'm sorry, but there has been an accident and…" Mrs C took a deep breath. "Jasmine Curson is dead."

5

8:50 PM, THURSDAY 31 DECEMBER

"Dead?" Blood pounded in Lady Beatrice's head. *Not dead, surely.*

"Yes, my lady. It looks like she slipped on some oil in the storage room and hit her head on the racking."

"But dead?" Perry Juke asked, grabbing Mrs Crammond's arm.

She patted his hand. "I'm sorry, Perry, but I checked. There was no pulse."

"Oh my giddy aunt!" Perry mumbled as he shook his head.

"Indeed." *Poor girl.*

"I was trying to find the inspector, you know the thickset one with short grey hair who was here investigating Alex Sterling's murder back in the spring? I thought I saw him here earlier with you, my lady, but I can't find him now."

Lady Beatrice sighed. Was it serendipity that Detective Inspector Mike Ainsley from Fenshire CID was here tonight or merely a coincidence? When she'd invited him, she'd been really pleased he'd said yes. With him having investigated three murders in the area over the last year, he felt like a permanent fixture at Francis Court. *Well, I'm glad he's here now.*

"Yes, Mrs C, Inspector Ainsley is here. You're right, we'll need to find him. Why don't you do that while Perry and I go to where the body is? Please be discreet though. I don't want to upset anyone and spoil the party. Was it you who found her?"

Mrs Crammond shook her head as she followed Lady Beatrice, Daisy, and Perry Juke. "No, my lady. Aaron Everett, the chef, found her. He went to get a saucepan, and there she was, dead on the floor."

"Does anyone else know?" Perry asked over his shoulder.

"He came straight out and found Leo and Holly, who were nearby."

Lady Beatrice gasped. *Oh no, poor Holly.* Finding out her sister was dead like that. And Leo, Jasmine's boyfriend, must be beside himself. "Where are they now?"

"I told them not to touch anything or let anyone in the room and came straight away to find the policeman. I wasn't sure what else to do, my lady. We don't have radios on a night like tonight and..."

Lady Beatrice turned and gave the housekeeper a smile. *What else can I do? Let's just hope it's a straightforward accident, or else, they have badly compromised the crime scene*. She grimaced and checked herself. *Of course it's an accident.* She was letting what had happened over the last nine months influence her thinking. *I'm seeing murder everywhere now!* "It's okay, Mrs C. You did the right thing."

They reached the corner of the Painted Hall. Mrs Crammond turned away from them towards the Salon while she and Perry headed towards the wooden door with 'Private' on it on their right, which led to the kitchen area.

Perry rushed along the corridor, texting as he walked.

Lady Beatrice hobbled after him. "Are you texting Simon?" She wished Perry's other-half Simon was here rather than in bed with the man flu. They needed him in a situation like this. And not just because he was an ex-detective sergeant; but he was the calming presence both she and Perry relied on.

"Yes," he said, stopping in front of the door leading to the kitchens. "But he's not replying. He must be asleep. Should I ring him?"

She caught up with him, and placing her hand on his arm, she took her shoes off. *Ah, that's better...* "No, let him sleep. We can tell him all about it later." She wiggled her toes to get some feeling into them, then took a deep breath. "Let's go in."

He nodded and opened the door.

They hurried down the corridor, past the brightly-lit kitchen and along to where she could see Holly Curson huddled next to a tall slim man she assumed was Leo Pack. Also standing with them was another man dressed in chef's whites. She presumed he was Aaron Everett.

As they approached, Holly was sobbing on Leo's shoulder while the chef stared at the door to the storage room as if in a trance.

Her stomach fluttered as she stopped in front of them. "Holly, I'm so sorry to hear about the accident."

The woman raised her head from Leo's shoulder and wiped her face just as Daisy jumped up at the couple, sniffing them both. "Daisy!" Lady Beatrice grabbed her little dog. "I'm so sorry," she said, holding Daisy in her arms. "Mrs Crammond has gone to fetch the police. They'll be here any minute. Can I suggest the three of you sit down in the kitchen area, and we'll come and find you soon?"

The three of them shuffled off towards the kitchen. She put Daisy down on the floor and turned to Perry. "Ready?"

He swallowed and nodded. "Daisy, stay here," she told her little dog as she dropped her shoes on the floor by the wall, and picking up her dress with one hand, she slowly turned the handle with the other. Her heart pounded as she and Perry entered the storage room.

The harsh light lit up the small room, its floor-to-ceiling racking on the other three walls making it feel cramped. Even though she'd seen more dead bodies this last year than she ever wanted to, she felt nauseous when looking down at the body in the red dress laying on the floor. Jasmine had her back resting at the bottom of the racking on Lady Beatrice's right-hand side, her head twisted slightly as it lay against the metal legs. To the left of her feet on the floor was what remained of a smashed bottle. Oil pooled around the shattered pieces of glass. Perry stepped past her, careful where he put his feet and, leaning over, rested his fingers on her neck. After a short while, he looked up and shook his head.

Moving forward, she looked a little closer. "There's no blood that I can see."

Perry stretched over the body and examined Jasmine's head. "No. There's a large red angry mark on the side of her head but nothing that has broken the skin." He stood up, being careful not to touch anything, and said, "It looks like she dropped a bottle of oil and slipped in it, hitting her head on the racking as she went down."

Lady Beatrice sniffed and tilted her head to one side. There was a deep nutty smell coming from somewhere. *It smelts like...* Still holding her dress, she bent down and looked at the bottle. Screwing up her eyes slightly, she read the label... *Sesame oil... That's it.* She straightened up, trying to recall the canapés being served this evening. She didn't think any of them used sesame oil. It was quite a distinctive flavour. *I wonder what she was doing with it in here*. Twisting her head, she looked down at Jasmine's feet. There was a smear of oil on the floor, and the light caught traces of oil on the heel of her right sandal. The left one was clean.

She stepped back. The way the body lay didn't look right. It made little sense. If she'd dropped the bottle of oil and then slipped in it, fallen backwards, hit her head, then twisted as she fell to rest where she was now, then she would have oil on her—

The door opened. She swung round. Detective Inspector Mike Ainsley stood in the doorway, his head blocking the light. "Lady Beatrice, Mr Juke. This wasn't how I was planning to spend New Year's Eve," he said with a wry smile.

Lady Beatrice turned to Perry. "Now that Mike has it under control, I'm going to pop upstairs, put some more comfortable shoes on, and quickly check on the boys. We're going to need a room for Mike to use and one for him to do interviews in. I'm thinking the Old Smoking Room and the Garden Room in the Events Suite will work. They have a connecting door that might be useful, and it's away from the ball so we can keep it quiet from the guests. Will you find Mrs C and get the keys to open them up? Also see if Ellie Gunn is around and can rustle up some coffee and tea for Jasmine's sister, her boyfriend, and the chef. They've all had a nasty shock. Just keep it discreet when you're talking to them."

Perry nodded. "Righty ho, leave it with me."

Lady Beatrice looked around. *Where's Daisy gone? She was here a minute ago...*

"Daisy!"

She walked towards the kitchen and poked her head around the first open door. *Daisy!* The little terrier had her front legs up against the side of a tall bin, trying to get her head in it.

"Daisy! Come here," Lady Beatrice cried.

Leo Pack and Holly Curson appeared from the open doorway leading into the kitchen area, looking quizzically at her.

How embarrassing. My dog is scavenging in kitchen bins!

"I'm so sorry," Lady Beatrice said, scooping up Daisy. "The police are here now and I'm sure they'll be out to see you shortly."

She hastened from the room. "I don't believe you sometimes, Daisy," she scolded the little terrier. "It's not like you don't get fed."

Perry moved up the corridor to meet her. "What happened?"

Lady Beatrice handed Daisy to a rather surprised-looking Perry. "Don't ask. But can you do me a favour, please? Look after her while I pop upstairs will you?"

"Of course," Perry replied, patting Daisy resting comfortably in his arms.

"And don't let her anywhere near the kitchens!" was Lady Beatrice's parting shot as she headed away from him down the corridor.

Fifteen minutes later in shoes that didn't hurt her feet and satisfied that the two boys hadn't killed themselves or each other, Lady Beatrice entered the Old Smoking Room to find Mike Ainsley already there, perched on the arm of a blue sofa, his mobile phone up against his ear.

"A couple of hours at the least? Well, do you know where Hines is?" He looked up at her as she walked towards him and rolled his eyes. "Well, please keep trying. And when you do find him, ask him to ring me ASAP, please? Thank you." He cut the call. "Well that's a pain. They can't get hold of Detective Sergeant Hines, and there's been a major incident in Kings Town, so everyone is tied up there at the moment. They hope they can get someone to us in the next few hours."

Lady Beatrice sighed. "We'll just have to wait, I guess."

He stood up and shook his head. "I don't think that's a good idea. We need to get statements as soon as possible. If we leave it, then there's a chance that witnesses will forget what they saw. Evidence will be lost. I think it's best I start the investigation now. I might need your and Mr Juke's help. After all, you have both been, shall we say, 'involved' in several investigations over the last year, so you know the dos and don'ts."

He grinned at her, and she blushed. Their involvement in three previous murder investigations this year had been a sore point for some, although Mike had always appreciated their help.

"Yes, of course. Do you think you can keep it as low-key as possible though, Mike? I don't want to disturb the guests—"

"I'll do my best, my lady. I assume most of the guests don't have access to the kitchen area?"

She nodded. "Only Sophie Crammond and Ellie Gunn are involved with tonight's organisation."

"Okay, Lady Beatrice. Then let's start with the people who worked with the victim, shall we?" He smiled tentatively.

She smiled back. "Thank you." *Hold on. Did he say victim?* "Don't you think this is a straightforward accident then?"

He tilted his head to one side. “What was your first impression of the scene when you entered the storage room?”

“It didn’t make any sense to me,” she told him, frowning. “The oil was on the wrong heel.”

He raised an eyebrow. “Continue.”

“Well, if Jasmine had slipped on the oil where it was on the floor, then in order to land where she did, she would have had to step in it with her left foot, but her left shoe had no oil on it.” She looked at him. He was listening. She continued, “And I also don’t understand why there was no blood. All the shelves on the racking stick out, and they’re very thin. If she hit one of them, then surely there would be a large cut, more like a slice, that would have broken the skin?”

She waited for his response. He slowly smiled. “Well observed. I had similar concerns. So I sent some photos to Forensics and got someone there to have a look at them for me. They believe someone hit the victim on the top side of her head with something large and blunt. They agree that the shelves or posts of the units would have created a smaller and deeper wound.”

“So maybe one of the pots or pans in there?”

He shrugged. “Maybe. The scene of crime officers will go through everything in the room to see if it contains traces of the victim. Of course, it’s also possible that the weapon was taken out of the room and disposed of or cleaned.”

“By the way, did you notice the smell? It was sesame oil. I can’t imagine why Jasmine would have been carrying sesame oil. It’s used mainly in Oriental cookery, and none of the food has those flavours tonight. The theme is Hollywood, so it’s mostly American food.”

“Interesting. I didn’t make that connection. We’ll need to ask the chef. But like you, I also noticed there was only oil on her right heel and so asked my contact in Forensics his view.

He confirmed that unless the victim had somehow pivoted one hundred and eighty degrees between hitting the oil and landing, then she should have oil on her left shoe as well."

"So you think someone staged it to look like she'd slipped on the oil?"

He nodded. "I think it's more likely than not that this is murder, and someone has tried to make it look like an accident."

"Oh my giddy aunt!" Perry Juke walked into the room, Daisy by his side. "Did you just say that Jasmine Curson was murdered?"

6

9:15 PM, THURSDAY 31 DECEMBER

"So, Mr Everett, you say you went to the storage room to get a small saucepan, and that's when you found Jasmine Curson's body. Is that correct?"

Aaron Everett, sitting opposite Mike Ainsley on the edge of a large blue velvet Chesterfield in the Garden Room, wiped his hands down the front of his white jacket and nodded. "Yes."

"And what time was that?" Mike, sitting in an armchair with a piece of paper resting on the back of a book, had his pen poised to record his reply.

"Eight-thirty."

He wrote it down. "And how do you know it was eight-thirty, Mr Everett?"

The man shifted slightly in his chair. "There's a clock in the kitchen, and I was monitoring it. We were due to stop serving hot food at eight-thirty."

"I see. So if you were stopping serving food at eight-thirty, why did you need a saucepan?"

Lady Beatrice, sitting off to the side of the two men, raised an eyebrow. *That's a good question.* She still couldn't quite believe Mike was allowing her to sit in on the interviews. He'd said it would help put people at ease.

"I said we were stopping serving *hot* food, sir. I needed to make a chocolate sauce to drizzle over the individual profiteroles waiting to go out."

"I see. So what did you do when you discovered Miss Curson on the floor?"

The chef raised his hands to his face and mumbled something Lady Beatrice couldn't hear.

"I didn't catch that, Mr Everett. Can you repeat what you just said, please?"

Aaron Everett slumped forwards as he removed his trembling hands from his face. "I panicked. She was laying there. I thought she was dead." He slowly shook his head. "And I didn't know what to do. So I ran out of the room. I think I was shouting. Leo and Holly came running towards me. I told them what I'd seen, and Holly told me to find Mrs Crammond, who would probably be in the Painted Hall by the food tables, and that's what I did."

"So you touched nothing in the storage room?"

He looked down at his hands now clasped in his lap and shook his head.

There's something bothering him. She felt sure of it. *Jasmine employed Aaron without getting Holly's agreement,* she recalled. Maybe he was worried he would lose his job now…

"And when did you last see Jasmine Curson alive?"

Aaron shrugged but didn't raise his head. "I can't remember. I was too busy in the kitchen to keep tabs on what everyone else was doing."

"And is that where you were all evening?"

"Yes. Getting out hot food for so many is hard work, you know."

"Okay. Thank you, Mr Everett. That will be all for now. Please stay in the kitchen area for the time being."

"Can I just ask one thing, please?" Both men turned to Lady Beatrice. Mike raised an eyebrow. *Well, I'm sorry, but you forgot to ask...* "Aaron, did any of the dishes tonight use sesame oil?"

Frowning, Aaron shook his head slowly.

"Any idea why Jasmine would have sesame oil with her when she was found?"

"No. It wasn't there earlier, so it must have come from the pantry. But I've no idea..."

"All right, well thank you, anyway." She smiled at the chef.

He nodded and slouched out of the room.

Perry popped his head around the connecting door. "Who do you want next?"

"Er, Leo Pack, I think," Mike said.

"I'm on it," Perry replied as his head disappeared.

Mike smiled, then looked over at Lady Beatrice. "What do you think?"

"I think he's either not telling us something, or he's worried about losing his job."

"Why would he be concerned about that?"

She quickly filled him in on the conversation she'd had with Perry two days ago.

"So things weren't all roses and unicorns in Posh and Fabulous then? Good, that gives us a motive."

———

"So, Mr Pack. You say you were concerned because Jasmine Curson hadn't turned up to meet you as planned in one of the back offices before you were both due to do your meet and greet?"

Jasmine's boyfriend nodded.

"So why did you go to the kitchens to look for her? Did you think that's where she would be?"

Leo shrugged. "I'd already had a look in the Salon and the ballroom, so I thought she might be in the back area talking to Holly." His voice was monotone and flat.

He'll still be in shock, hardly able to believe that Jasmine is gone. As someone who had lost her husband fifteen years ago in a car accident, Lady Beatrice could sympathise with that feeling of numbness and disbelief.

"So tell us what happened when you got to the kitchen area, please."

Leo rubbed the side of his face and frowned. "Well, just as I opened the door from the Painted Hall to the kitchens, I bumped into Leah, you know, the serving supervisor. I asked her if she'd seen Jas, and she said no and suggested maybe she was in the foyer with guests. So I asked her if Holly was there, and she said she thought so and offered to get her for me while I quickly checked if Jas was in the foyer. I did that. When I still couldn't find her, I went back to the door, and Holly appeared. I told her I'd searched everywhere, and the only place she could be was somewhere in the back. Holly said that maybe I'd missed her, and she was now waiting for me in the office. You can get to the office from that door, so we went through. As we did, we heard a shout. Holly ran towards the kitchen, and I followed. That's when I saw Aaron running towards us shouting that there'd been a dreadful accident, and he thought Jas was dead." He put his hand to his mouth and let out a moan.

"Do you know what time that was, Mr Pack?"

Leo Pack raised watery eyes to DI Ainsley and shook his

head. “I started looking for Jas at about twenty past eight, so I suppose it was ten or fifteen minutes later.”

“Thank you. And then what did you do?”

He sniffed and wiped his eyes. “Holly told Aaron to get Mrs C, then we went into the storage room.” His Adam’s apple bobbed up and down as he took a deep breath. “I could tell she was dead. Her head was sort of twisted—” He stopped. Mike poured a glass of water from the jug Perry had thoughtfully arranged on the table between them, along with six upturned glasses, and handed it to Leo. He took a sip, then continued, “Holly made a noise and grabbed at the racking, so I tried to help her steady herself, then Mrs Crammond came in and told us not to touch anything and to come back out. I waited with Holly and Aaron outside the door while Mrs Crammond went to get help.”

“Thank you, Mr Pack. Did you touch anything while you were inside the storage room with Holly Curson?”

He hesitated slightly, then shook his head. “No,” he said firmly.

Lady Beatrice frowned. *Why the hesitation? Is he hiding something too?*

“And when did you last see Jasmine Curson alive?”

Leo puffed out his cheeks. “I don’t know. About seven forty-five, I think? We were at the bar, and she got a call. Then she said she needed to do something, but she wouldn’t be long and would meet me in the office to get changed for the meet and greet. She told me not to be late, then disappeared.”

“And do you know who the call was from?”

He shook his head. “It only lasted a few seconds. She listened, then said, ‘Okay.’ That’s it.”

Mike wrote something down on his sheet of paper. “And what did you do after she left?”

"Erm, I finished my drink, then went to sit in the office at the back and watch some TikTok stuff while I waited for her. Then when she still hadn't arrived at twenty past eight, I left, as I've already told you."

"And did you see anyone while you were in the office waiting for Miss Curson?"

He shook his head. "No."

"Thank you, Mr Pack." Mike looked up at her. "Lady Beatrice, do you have questions?"

She raked through her mind to see if there was anything she thought Mike had forgotten. *Motive!*

"Just a quick question, Leo. How did you feel when Jasmine bought Aaron Everett into the business? Did she tell you in advance what she was doing?"

Leo Pack's mouth fell open for a second, then he closed it and said in a halting voice, "No. She didn't tell me. But then it was her and Holly's business, nothing to do with me, so why would she?" He met her gaze briefly, then looked away.

"I understand Holly was quite upset when she found out. Did she and Jasmine have an argument about it?"

Leo shrugged. "I don't know. It was between her and Jas. I didn't get involved." He folded his arms across his chest and leaned back in his seat.

That's not what Perry said! But it was clear he wasn't going to say any more. She nodded at Mike, and he thanked Leo for his help and asked him to wait in the kitchen area with the others.

As the door closed, Perry once again stuck his head around the connecting door. "Don't tell me, you want to see Holly next?"

Mike nodded just as his phone rang.

Lady Beatrice rose and walked over to the window, the hem of her dress brushing the rug underneath her feet. Had someone really murdered Jasmine? And if so, which one of the people she'd worked with had killed her? Having seen Jasmine in action and knowing how she herself had taken an almost instant dislike to the woman, Lady Beatrice could believe that someone could've felt strongly enough to put a stop to her. Permanently.

As she turned back towards her seat, Mike ended the call. "That was Forensics. They're on their way here now. I've asked for them to arrive via the tradesmen's entrance and ask for Mrs Crammond. I've told them not to come in all guns blazing but to be discreet."

"Thank you. I'll ask Perry to warn Mrs Crammond. She should be able to meet them round the rear of the building and bring them in through the servants' hall."

The door opened, and Holly Curson walked in. Her eyes were swollen and puffy, and she looked pale in her midnight-blue evening dress. Poor woman. *This must be a huge shock for her.* Lady Beatrice gave her a sweet smile as she passed her and walked through the connecting door.

———

Walking back into the Garden Room some ten minutes later, Lady Beatrice was disturbed to see Holly sitting opposite Mike with her head in her hands, her shoulders heaving as she emitted a low moan. She looked at Mike. *What happened?* As if he could read her mind, he gave a little shrug, a bemused look on his face. She walked over to the sofa and sat down next to Holly. She reached over and poured a glass of water, then tapping her lightly on the shoulder, she offered her the cup.

"I'm so sorry, my lady. I just can't believe she's gone," she said as she grasped the cup and lifted it to her lips. She took a sip, then hiccuped as she placed the cup down on the table. After inhaling deeply, she slowly let the breath out through her mouth. "I'll be all right now."

Lady Beatrice smiled at her, then rose and returned to her chair by the window.

"Thank you, Miss Curson. You were explaining where you were when you heard Aaron shout."

"Yes," she said, her voice strained. "Leo and I were just inside the door when I heard a shout. I ran towards the kitchens, and there was Aaron. He was in a bit of a state. I could just make out that he said there had been an accident in the storage room, and he thought Jas was dead." After a sharp intake of breath, she grabbed the glass of water. Taking a sip, she carried on, "I told him to find Mrs Crammond. I ran into the room. Leo was with me. When I saw Jas laying there on the floor, I felt my legs give way. I grabbed the nearest bit of racking to steady myself. I think Leo tried to help. Then I remember Mrs Crammond was suddenly there. She took my arm and guided me and Leo out of the room. She told us to wait there and not let anyone into the room, then she ran off." Letting out a ragged breath, Holly wiped her face with the back of her hand.

"And you didn't touch anything or go back into the room again?" Mike asked.

She shook her head. Mike caught Lady Beatrice's eye and raised an eyebrow.

"Holly. Just a quick question. I understand it was Jasmine who employed Aaron, the chef, a while back without telling you. Is that true?" Lady Beatrice asked.

Holly Curson put down the cup of water and turned to look at Lady Beatrice. She tilted her head to one side. "Yes, she did."

"And how did you react?"

She rubbed her hands up her arms. "I was a little upset at first. We normally discuss any decision to employ anyone first. But our previous chef had just resigned, and Jas explained she was worried we would be without a chef, so when she discovered Aaron in a restaurant in London, and he was up for a change, so she said she'd acted quickly. Once I understood that she'd done it for the good of the business, I was fine about it."

"Thank you, Holly." *Do I believe her?* She wasn't sure. It seemed plausible, at least.

"I have one last question, please, Miss Curson," Mike said. "Where were you between seven forty-five and eight-thirty this evening?"

Holly Curson stiffened. She ran her hands down the skirt of her dress. "I can't be very precise, inspector. I was so busy making sure everything was running smoothly, but I think I was over by the food tables at one point, making sure the fondue wasn't running dry. Then I went outside to have a vape and then back to the kitchens and did a little washing up as it was piled high and Leah wasn't there. I think that's about it."

"And did you see anyone during that time?"

"Well, obviously I saw lots of guests, but I don't recall I spoke to anyone in particular. While I was outside, I saw someone sitting down in one of the back offices. I think it was Leo. He was tall and thin, just like him. And I spoke to Leah when she came in to tell me that Leo was looking for me." She rubbed her hands together and smiled.

"Thank you, Miss Curson. That's all for now, but we may need to talk to you again this evening, so please remain on the premises."

She rose. She nodded to Lady Beatrice and left the room.

Lady Beatrice stood up, and stretching her neck from side

to side, she walked over to where Mike had also risen. "So we think the time of death is between seven forty-five, when Jasmine was last seen by Leo at the bar, and eight-thirty, when Aaron found her body?"

He nodded. "Yes, although it's likely that Forensics can narrow it down further once they do the autopsy. But at the moment I think that's the time frame we need to concentrate on."

"Indeed." She poured herself a glass of water and took a sip. "Leo mentioned Jasmine took a call before she left him. I don't recall seeing a phone in the room, do you?"

Mike shook his head. "I didn't search her though. I didn't have any gloves on me."

Her phone beeped, and she walked over to pick it up. *Rats!* It was a message from Mrs C saying that people were asking where she was and what should she tell them. She sighed. She'd have to put in an appearance, or they would work out something was wrong. "I'm really sorry, Mike, but I need to show my face at the ball, or people will wonder what's going on."

"Of course, my lady. I'll see the other two employees now, and I hope by then Forensics will have arrived and we'll have a bit more to go on. You go, and we'll catch up later."

7

10:15 PM, THURSDAY 31 DECEMBER

Throwing herself down on the sofa by the French doors in the Old Smoking Room, Lady Beatrice pulled off her shoes and rubbed her toes. Daisy jumped up next to her and nuzzled her mistress. "Oh, Daisy, even these shoes are hurting now," she told her furry companion as she gave her a quick peck on the head.

"I think I've had too much cheese," Perry Juke said, slumping down in one of the two armchairs opposite her. "There's a good reason why fondues went out of fashion back in the seventies, you know." He undid his jacket button and puffed out his cheeks.

Daisy jumped off the sofa and trotted towards the door as Inspector Mike Ainsley walked into the room, closing the door behind him. He stopped to greet the little terrier, then moved to close the connecting door.

"You two look done in," he said as he sat in the other chair opposite Lady Beatrice.

"Being sociable is overrated," she said with a smile as Daisy joined her on the sofa.

He smiled back. "Well, while you two were entertaining

your guests, I've been with the Forensics team at the crime scene."

She and Perry perked up. "And?" Perry asked.

"Well, firstly, they've confirmed that the victim died from blunt force trauma. She didn't hit her head on the racking. They have also confirmed, due to the placement of the body and the oil on her shoe and on the floor, that she didn't slip on the oil."

Lady Beatrice leaned back and sighed. "So nothing new then?"

"I haven't finished yet. Under the racking by the door was a small piece of dried mango." He unlocked his phone screen and showed them both the pictures.

"Why is that relevant?" Perry asked. "It could have been there for months."

"I spoke to Mrs Crammond, the head housekeeper, and Ellie Gunn, the catering manager. They both said that the storage room, along with all the cooking areas were deep cleaned yesterday, ready for the event. So it must have appeared since then. They found an almost full box in the pantry, so it seems likely it came from there."

Lady Beatrice frowned. *That's odd. How would one random piece have got from the pantry to the storage room?* "Aaron might shed some light on it," she offered.

"Yes, I'll ask him." He tipped his head, then said, "Oh, and they also retrieved Jasmine Curson's mobile phone. It was in a small pocket of her dress."

Lady Beatrice shifted forward on the sofa. "And who was it that rung her when she was with Leo?"

"It was our chef, Aaron Everett."

"So is he now our number one suspect?" Perry asked eagerly.

"He certainly didn't tell us about making that call, so that's suspicious," Mike replied.

Aaron. So is that what he was being cagey about? Had he met up with Jasmine in the storage room? But why would he kill her?

"Do you think they were an item?" Perry asked them. "After all, she brought him into the firm without agreeing on it with anyone else."

Mike put his mobile back in his pocket. "It's possible, that's for sure. I think we need to get him back and see what he has to say for himself."

"How did you get on with Leah?" Lady Beatrice asked him.

"Not much from her. She said she was looking after the serving staff and was backwards and forwards between the kitchen and the foyer where they were serving the last round of canapés. She confirmed Aaron Everett was in the kitchen from about eight-fifteen to eight-thirty as they'd had a chat while they'd waited for the servers to bring the empty trays back. Before that time, she was vague. She also confirmed both Leo's story, that she went to get Holly for him, and that Holly Curson was washing up when she found her."

Lady Beatrice sighed. "So that means Aaron doesn't have an alibi for the time of death?"

"Not all of it. Mr Juke, would you be kind enough to get him for me, please?"

Perry stood up. "Yes, of course. I won't be a tick."

8

10:30 PM, THURSDAY 31 DECEMBER

Lady Beatrice studied Aaron Everett slouching on the sofa in front of Mike Ainsley as he stared at the floor, his left leg jerking up and down until he placed his hand on his knee. *What's he so nervous about? Did he kill Jasmine?*

Mike took out his pen, and with it hovering over the now almost full page of notes, he addressed the chef. "So Mr Everett, I need to ask you a few more questions—"

"Look, what's this all about? I know you want to know about Jas's movements before she died. But why are we all being kept here? And who are the guys in the white suits?" He rubbed the back of his head and huffed. "I want to know what's going on!"

Was Mike going to tell him he thought someone had murdered Jasmine? Or would he continue to keep that to himself for a bit longer?

"We don't believe that Miss Curson's death was a straightforward accident."

Aaron gasped, raising his hand to his mouth.

Slightly cryptic, but it seems to have had the effect he

wanted. The chef, who had turned pale, looked genuinely shocked.

He dropped his hand from his mouth. "You mean someone killed her?" His eyes darted from Mike to Lady Beatrice and back.

"We believe so," Mike answered.

Aaron shook his head, then slumped back on the sofa.

"We know you called Jasmine at seven forty-five this evening. What was the call about?"

Aaron heaved a sigh. "I was telling her I was free."

"Free?"

"I had a few minutes with nothing to do."

"So you arranged to meet her, did you?"

He hung his head and nodded.

"Were you and Jasmine Curson having an affair, Mr Everett?"

Again he nodded.

This is like pulling teeth!

"Mr Everett." Mike raised his voice.

The chef looked up.

"I need you to tell me exactly what happened, please."

Lady Beatrice leaned forward.

He sighed. "I met Jas a few months ago. I was working in a restaurant that belonged to a friend of hers, and we just hit it off straight away. She was ambitious and exciting, so when she asked me to come and work for Posh and Fabulous as head chef, I jumped at the chance. Our affair began within a few days of my first event." He ran his fingers through his short brown hair. "I suppose I always knew that's what she wanted when she offered me the job. And" —he shrugged— "she was an attractive woman with lots of connections."

Lady Beatrice suppressed a sigh. *Do people really use each other like that? How sad...*

"Anyway. We grabbed time together when we could, mainly when we were working. I don't think either of us had any expectations. She was with Leo. He has money, so she wasn't going to leave him. I didn't care. It was just a bit of fun…"

"So what happened tonight?" Mike prompted.

"I rang her to say I was free and to meet me in the storage cupboard. I told the kitchen staff I was going to get some more ingredients for dessert from the pantry."

Mango?

"I popped in there, grabbed the first thing I found, then went to the storage cupboard to wait for her."

Lady Beatrice couldn't help herself. "Was it dried mango you grabbed?"

He nodded. "Yes. I opened the packet while I was waiting and ate a piece. I'm partial to mango."

"And then?" Mike's voice had an edge of impatience now.

"Jas turned up. We had a bit of fun, you know. Then I heard Leah calling for me, so I left sharp-ish like."

"What time was this?"

"The clock said ten past eight when I got back into the kitchen…" He trailed off, his voice breaking. He hung his head. "That was the last time I saw her alive."

"And what happened to the box of mango, Mr Everett?" Mike asked.

Aaron frowned. "I took it back to the pantry later."

But where had the piece that had been on the floor come from? "Did you drop any mango on the floor while you were in there?" she asked.

He turned to look at her, looking sheepish. "We knocked the box, and I cleaned it up after we were done. Guess I missed a piece."

"Okay, well thank you, Mr Everett. We will need to take a formal statement later, so you'll need to stay on-site until then, please."

"So do you think he did it?" Lady Beatrice asked Mike Ainsley as Perry walked in through the connecting door.

"Well, he was the last one to see her alive, *and* he found the body."

She sensed a but… "But?"

"His reaction when I told him it was murder seemed genuine. Plus, if he is telling the truth about the timing, then he has an alibi from eight-fifteen onwards."

Perry sat down with them. "If he and Jas were having an affair, maybe they had a lovers' tiff, and he lost it with her, grabbed a saucepan from one of the shelves, and walloped her over the head. It wouldn't take more than a few minutes to do that."

"But then, what about the oil?" Lady Beatrice pointed out. "He wouldn't have had time to get that, presumably from the pantry, and make it look like an accident."

Perry sighed. "I hadn't thought about that."

"What about Leo Pack? Do you think he could have done it?" Lady Beatrice asked. "If he knew about Jasmine's affair with Aaron, he would also have a strong motive to kill her?"

"Yes. Agreed. And then there's Holly. She said she was outside vaping, but no one saw her."

Hold on, though. "But didn't she say she saw Leo while she was outside? Wouldn't that give them both an alibi?"

Mike frowned and took his notes out of his pocket. Smoothing down the pieces of paper, he read them. "Yes, you're right. Here it is. She said she'd seen someone sitting down in one of the back offices. She said she thought it was Leo and that the person was tall and thin, just like him."

Lady Beatrice sank back in her chair. They seemed to be running towards a brick wall. She so wanted to get this resolved quickly and quietly without a large police presence to upset the guests and ruin the ball.

A phone beeped, and Mike Ainsley picked up his mobile. He looked at the message. "It's DS Hines. He's on his way. I want to give him an update, so do you mind if I just stretch my legs and call him? I think we need to re-interview Holly Curson and Leo Pack. Can you find them for me, Mr Juke, and bringing them in here? I'll be back shortly."

"Yes, sure," Perry said.

9

10:40 PM, THURSDAY 31 DECEMBER

Lady Beatrice rounded the corner, the coffee tray balanced in her hands, and walked past the Events Suite's dining room. She stopped. Daisy, just behind her, stopped too. Was that raised voices she could hear? They seemed to be coming from the corridor ahead. She sped up, and as she turned the corridor, the voices became more distinct. They were coming from the Garden Room where they'd left Holly and Leo. She paused. *Should I carry on and interrupt them?* She glanced at the open door of the Old Smoking Room. *Or should I pop in and see if I can hear them through the connecting door?* She hesitated for only a second more before pushing the door to the Old Smoking Room open further, and being as quiet as she could, she placed the tray carefully on the sideboard. Turning to Daisy, just by her side, she pointed to the armchair by the window. "Daisy, lie down," she whispered. Daisy trotted over and jumped up onto the chair. She circled twice, then plonked herself down and, curling up, closed her eyes. Lady Beatrice tip-toed over to the large wooden connecting door. She put her ear up against the slight gap where the door met the frame and listened.

"So why *did* you say you saw me when you didn't? I was in that office they gave us to get changed in waiting for Jas. You couldn't have seen me from outside if you were on the other side of the house." Leo Pack's voice was shaky and raised.

"I was just trying to help, Leo." Holly Curson sounded close to tears. "It's clear from what Aaron said that this is now a murder enquiry, and it's possible the police will think you killed Jas. If you have an alibi, then they will leave you alone."

"Me? Me kill Jas? Is that what you think? Why would I want to do that? I loved her." He was quieter now, and Lady Beatrice had to strain to hear him.

"I know. But the police don't care about that. They need a suspect, and you're the perfect—"

"Why?" Leo jumped in. "Why would the police think I would want to hurt Jas?"

"Maybe they know you guys argued earlier this evening."

"So? It was just a minor disagreement. Jas wanted to bring our trip to Costa Rica forward, and I said no because I have a modelling engagement booked. She couldn't understand why I wouldn't just cancel, but I didn't want to let them down. It would be unprofessional."

Despite his casual rich-boy persona, it seems he has a solid work ethic.

"Was that all you argued about?" Holly sounded sceptical.

"Yes. She eventually accepted that we needed to stick to the original leaving date, and although she wasn't especially happy about it, we were fine after that."

"So you didn't argue about Aaron then? I thought you would be mad about it?"

So Holly knew about Aaron, did she? Why didn't she say anything to us?

"Aaron? The chef? Why would we argue about him?"

It was quiet. Lady Beatrice held her breath.

"Holly? Why aren't you saying anything?" Leo sounded apprehensive.

"I'm sorry, Leo. I thought you knew..." Holly's voice was unsteady.

"Knew what?" Leo asked urgently. "What's going on, Holly?"

Lady Beatrice could just hear Holly sigh. "Aaron and Jas were having a fling."

There was silence in the other room.

The tension seeped into her bones as she inched silently closer...

When a hand suddenly touched her shoulder, Lady Beatrice jumped out of her skin. She swung round, raising her arm, about to strike out at the assailant. He sprung backwards, his hands up in front of him. *Perry!* She let out a breath and lowered her hand to her chest. "You frightened the life out of me," she hissed.

"Sorry," he whispered. "What's going on?"

Her heartbeat beginning to slow, she put her forefinger against her lips and pointed to the connecting door with her other hand. She leaned back against the wood. *Did I miss anything?* Perry too leaned against the door, just above her.

"How long have you known?" Leo asked in a dull voice.

"I've seen them sneaking around together ever since he got here. I confronted her about it this evening..." Holly's voice trailed off.

There was silence.

"So do you see now why I tried to give you an alibi, Leo? If they even think you knew about the affair, that gives you motive. I just wanted to—"

"Help? Well, thanks, Holly. You've been a tremendous

help," he bit back at her. "You've just told me that the woman I loved had been deceiving me for months with some jumped-up chef who thinks he's Gordon Ramsey." His voice got louder. "Well, thank you for that!" he shouted as his footsteps quickened on the wooden floor.

Rats! He's leaving...

Grabbing Perry's jacket sleeve, Lady Beatrice pulled him away from the door and towards the sofas by the French doors. "Get down," she muttered under her breath as she dragged him behind the nearest sofa and ducked.

Holding her breath, Lady Beatrice sat on the floor staring at Perry while he stared back. Footsteps in the corridor outside the open door suggested they had hidden just in time. As the heavy steps faded, there was a thud, and Daisy peered around the edge of the back of the sofa, her tail wagging. They burst out laughing.

"Well, that was close," Perry said, scrambling up off the floor and holding out his hand to her. "Indeed," she said, taking his hand and allowing him to pull her up.

"So I take it from the snippet I heard that Holly deliberately made up an alibi to protect Leo because she'd thought he'd known about Aaron and Jasmine and killed her because of it?"

She nodded as she brushed down her dress and patted her up-do. "Pretty much. Leo said he didn't know about the affair, but I'm not too sure if I believe him. He didn't actually deny that he knew. He just turned it around on Holly. Either way, we need to tell Mike before he interviews them."

Lady Beatrice: *Just found out Leo doesn't have an alibi.*

. . .

Mike: *Okay. I'll be there in a minute.*

10

11:15 PM, THURSDAY 31 DECEMBER

"Sorry to keep you waiting, Holly." Lady Beatrice, followed by Perry and Daisy, entered the Garden Room, carrying a tray of coffee. Holly Curson, who had leapt up from the blue Chesterfield sofa while wiping her eyes, mumbled, "That's fine."

Lady Beatrice placed the tray down on the coffee table as Daisy ran across the room and jumped up at Holly.

"Daisy!" Lady Beatrice admonished. "Get down now!" Daisy, who was sniffing at the small bag slung low across Holly's upper body, tilted her head to one side and reluctantly let her paws drop to the floor. "I'm so sorry, Holly. She's no respecter of personal space, I'm afraid," Lady Beatrice said, smiling.

Holly nodded, staring down at the little dog now sitting by the side of the sofa.

"Would you like a coffee?"

Holly nodded.

Lady Beatrice picked up the coffee pot, pleased to feel it was still hot, and poured the black liquid into a cup. "Do sit down, Holly, and help yourself to milk and sugar. Perry, do you want one?" She looked up and caught Perry's eye. Shaking his head, he moved to sit on the armchair adjacent to Holly.

Lady Beatrice glanced at the door as she heard heavy footsteps in the corridor.

Mike Ainsley entered the room and strode across to where she was standing. Daisy moved to sit next to him, and he bent down briefly to pat her head. "Coffee, inspector?" she offered with a smile.

He gave her a quick nod, leaned back against the arm of the chair, and addressed Holly Curson. "Sorry to keep you waiting, Miss Curson, but I have a few more questions, if you don't mind?"

Holly clasped her hands together. "Um, yes, of course."

"Why did you tell us you saw Leo Pack in the back office when you clearly didn't?"

Well, that's direct. Lady Beatrice handed Mike a black coffee and perched on the arm of the chair Perry was sitting in. She draped her arm over the back. Holly, meanwhile, shifted in her seat. *Is she going to admit it?*

"Well, I just wanted to help him. I knew he couldn't kill anyone, but I was worried you would arrest him if he didn't have an alibi. I couldn't let that happen." She blushed and looked down at her hands, wringing them together.

"So you were lying?" Mike clarified. She nodded her head without looking up.

"You also didn't tell us about Aaron and Jasmine's affair. Why?"

Holly sat up straight and lifted her chin. "I didn't think Aaron would say anything, and I didn't want my sister's reputation ruined over a brief fling... " She shot up out of her seat. "Why are you asking me all these questions? I've just lost my sister..." She threw herself back onto the sofa and buried her face in her hands.

Lady Beatrice looked at Mike. She knew he needed to ask these questions before interviewing Leo so he could better catch him in a lie, but he was being a bit heavy-handed. Lady Beatrice rose and went to open her mouth to reassure the woman that these were just routine questions when Daisy jumped up on the sofa next to Holly and poked her head into the poor woman's lap.

"Daisy!" Lady Beatrice lurched forward to grab her naughty terrier, but Mike got there first and blocked her path.

"What are you up to, Daisy?" he said, standing over Holly and leaning in.

Stop her! This was so embarrassing. Daisy was practically assaulting the poor woman.

Mike grabbed Daisy, then holding her in his arms, he said, "Miss Curson, do you have something in your bag?" She lifted her head from her hands and frowned. "Just my phone, some money, and lipstick."

"Would you mind letting me look, please?" He held his arm out.

Holly looked from him to Lady Beatrice and back. A pink rash began spreading up her neck. She held her hands over the bag. "I don't see why it's relevant?"

Why is she being difficult? Then she realised. *Maybe there's something feminine in there that she is embarrassed for him to see.* She stepped around Mike and leaned towards Holly. "If you'd rather, I can have a quick look inside?"

Holly's face was now blotchy with patches of raised red skin showing. She let go of the bag and pulled it over her head before handing it to Lady Beatrice with shaky hands. *I think we need to stop questioning her now. The woman is terrified.* She opened the clasp and peered inside. There was a small bundle of folded bank notes, a lipstick case, and a mobile phone. As she was about to close the bag, she recognised the faint smell of sesame oil and soap.

That's odd. She wouldn't have had her bag while she'd been washing up, so why grab it before going to see her sister?

Her eyes widened as another thought occurred to her. *She gave Leo an alibi before this was a murder investigation!* "Holly..."

Holly Curson let out a sob. "I didn't mean to kill her!" she cried and then buried her head in her hands again, her whole body shaking.

"Oh my giddy aunt," Perry muttered.

Just then, there was a knock on the door, and Detective Sergeant Eamon Hines and two uniformed officers walked into the room.

Ten minutes later, after Holly Curson had stopped sobbing enough for DS Hines to caution her, she started confessing to killing her sister Jasmine.

"I never meant to kill her, really. She's my sister, and I love her." She paused. "Loved her. But she wasn't always so loveable. She could be manipulative and cruel even. Especially when it came to Leo. But I didn't want to kill her. I just wanted to stop her from saying such vile things," she explained, sitting on the sofa, a glass of water in her hand. She took a sip, then looked up and met Lady Beatrice's gaze. "You must believe me. I never wanted her dead."

Resisting the urge to look away, she smiled at the woman. "Why don't you tell us exactly what happened, Holly?"

Holly raised a shaking hand to the side of her head and tucked her hair behind her ear. "I had my suspicions about her and Aaron for a few weeks now. I caught them whispering together at an event last weekend, and it was difficult to ignore the looks they exchanged. She also was snappy with Leo lately, and they were arguing a lot. Poor Leo, he really deserves better than to be treated the way she treated him…" She stopped and stared down at the glass in her hand.

"And so…" Lady Beatrice gently prompted her.

She looked up. "I suspected that something was going on between Jas and Aaron. About ten past eight tonight, I went to find her to check she had everything she needed ready to make her grand entrance with Leo at eight-thirty. I couldn't find her, and when I went into the kitchen, I noticed Aaron was missing too. I asked Leah where he was, and she said he had gone to look for some ingredients in the pantry. As I was walking out of the kitchen, I noticed him sneaking out of the storage room. I guessed he'd been in there with Jasmine. I was so mad, I barely waited for him to go into the kitchen before I rushed into the room and confronted her. She was standing there adjusting her dress, looking so smug that I just wanted to scream at her."

Holly cleared her throat, and after another sip of water, she continued, "I asked her what she was playing at cheating on Leo, and she told me she didn't love Leo." She shook her head, a tear rolling down her face. She wiped it away. "She stood there and admitted it to me. So I asked her why not just let him go then? Free him up to be with someone who would love him and make him happy. She just laughed! 'Who, you?' she sneered. 'Do you really think he would want to be with you when he's been with me? Sloppy seconds isn't his style, little sister.'" Holly took a shuddering breath. "Of course, everyone knew she was prettier and more outgoing than me. But did she really need to rub it in like that? I remember I had to clasp my hands together to stop myself from hitting her. I then challenged her about Aaron and asked her how she thought Leo would feel when he found out. She said, 'Leo won't ever know unless you say something. And you won't do that, little sis, will you? It would hurt him so much.' She told me Aaron was just a bit of fun and that she wasn't ready to give up Leo just yet because he paid for everything."

Holly shifted in her seat and put her water down. Her voice raised as she continued, "I pointed out that she had a good income from the business. She laughed in my face and said, 'Oh, little sis, you have no idea do you?' Then she rolled her eyes and sighed. 'Why would I spend my money when I can spend Leo's trust fund?' I was so mad at her. How could she use Leo like that? Poor Leo, so trusting, so in love with her. She didn't deserve him, you know." Her gaze met Lady Beatrice's. "She wasn't worthy of his love."

Her blue eyes glazed over, and she fell silent for a few seconds.

Then softly, she continued, "I don't really know what happened. The next thing I remember, I'm standing over Jas, who is laying on the floor, not moving. I looked at my hands. They were gripped around the handle of a black cast-iron frying pan. It felt heavy. I called her name, but nothing happened. Her eyes were closed. She wasn't moving. I started to shake. I didn't know what to do."

She raised her hand to her face and wiped away a tear. "Jas was on her back just at the bottom of a large steel built-in unit, her head twisted to one side. She looked like she'd fallen and hit her head. And that's when I thought that maybe I could cover it up and pretend it was an accident."

She sighed, not looking up, and continued, "It took me less than three minutes to leave the room, pop into the pantry, grab the first small bottle of oil I found, and rush back into the storage room. Using a hand towel, I moved to where Jas's feet were and poured some oil on the floor. I smeared it around and wiped some on the heel of her shoe. I was about to put the lid back on the oil when I realised it would look odd if the bottle wasn't there. Maybe she had the bottle in her hand, dropped it, then slipped? That would work. So I stood where I imagined she would have been and dropped the bottle." She flinched. "Then I picked up the frying pan and snuck out of the room. I had just finished washing it in the sink in the back kitchen when Leah came in and told me Leo was looking for me. I put the frying pan on the side to dry and went off to find him. He was concerned that it was almost eight-thirty and Jas hadn't turned up for them to do their meet and greet. I was worried he might be the one to find her, so I tried to put him off."

Lady Beatrice glanced over at Mike, who was leaning against the armchair where Daisy was curled up asleep, unaware of the drama unfolding opposite her. He cleared his throat. "And when you went back into the room later with Leo Pack, did you touch anything?"

She shook her head.

But why does her bag smell of oil and soap?

"And what did you do with the towel when you'd finished?" she asked.

"I took it back to the kitchen. I tried to wash it in the sink, and then I threw it in the bin. But then your dog…" She looked over at the sleeping Daisy. "Well, she was sniffing around, and I thought someone might find it. So I put it in my bag." She looked down at the floor and mumbled, "I was going to get rid of it when I got home…"

There was silence in the room, all eyes on the young woman who had just confessed to killing her sister. Sitting hunched up on the sofa, her head bent, her eyes closed, she looked so small and vulnerable. Lady Beatrice couldn't help hoping that she would be treated leniently when she was sentenced. She believed her about not meaning to kill Jasmine…

Mike Ainsley stood and moved towards Holly Curson. "Thank you for your frank and thorough account of what happened. I need you to accompany us to the police station, if you don't mind. A female constable will take you down to the car now." Holly rose, and Mike signalled to a uniformed policewoman, who walked over and gently took Holly's arm, leading her quietly out of the door.

Mike Ainsley turned to Lady Beatrice and Perry. "My lady, Mr Juke. Always a pleasure to see you. Although I'd prefer if it wasn't in such circumstances. Thank you for your help."

He was right. *How many times have I seen Mike this year? Three? No four now, including this one.* And each one had been related to a murder. *Am I a jinx?*

"Indeed, Mike. Although I'll be honest, this was the most straightforward investigation I've been involved with so far."

"Well, it always helps when you have a confession, my lady," he pointed out. "And it's different when it's a crime of passion rather than something premeditated. It was a rather sloppy attempt to cover up a murder, but that's what happens when they don't have time to think it through well enough beforehand." His lips twitched.

"Indeed. Well, I'll remember that when I want to kill someone, inspector. It's all about the planning." She grinned at him.

Perry snorted.

"Well, I need to be getting back to HQ and start the formal process with Miss Curson. Good night and" —Mike glanced at his watch— "as it's so close, can I wish you both a happy New Year."

"You too, Mike," she said as she watched him leave the room.

Perry coughed. "Actually, Bea, would you mind terribly if I disappeared now as well? I want to be with Simon at midnight." Perry shifted from one foot to another as if he was standing on hot coals.

Lady Beatrice cocked her head to one side. "But what about catching his cold and being ill?"

"I've decided I don't care. I can't leave him all on his own when the new year starts..." he said, looking sheepish. "Will you be okay on your own?"

She nodded. "Yes, I'll be fine. I'll go and hang out with Sam and Robbie upstairs as soon as I can get away." She grinned. "Go on then, and give him a big hug from me."

He slapped his hand to his chest. "I'm not going to touch him! He's diseased, remember?" Then he grinned back and leaned forward to kiss her on both cheeks, saying, "Happy New Year, Bea. May it be slightly less eventful than this one but equally as full of love and laughter."

She hugged him and in a shaky voice whispered, "It's been the best year ever as I bagged myself two very special friends in you and Simon."

He stepped back and then grinned. "I'll see you Sunday. Brunch at ours. Bring Sam and Robbie." With a wave, he disappeared through the door.

Lady Beatrice sighed, and crouching down as best she could in her dress, she leaned in and stroked Daisy's little white head. "Well, it's just you and me, Daisy-Doo. Which is fine by me." She stood up and looked at her watch. It was ten minutes to midnight. *I really should show my face at the party, and then I can join the boys.*

She walked towards the door. What a strange night it had been. *Maybe I should make a New Year's resolution this year... To stop finding any more dead bodies!*

11

EVENING, FRIDAY 1 JANUARY

The Society Page online article:

<u>Lady Beatrice and Her Son Join The King and Queen for Their Annual New Year's Day Lunch</u>

Fresh from hosting the annual Francis Court staff ball on New Year's Eve, Lady Beatrice (36), the Countess of Rossex, joined King James and Queen Olivia at their traditional New Year's Day lunch at their Fenshire home Fenn House. Lady Beatrice was accompanied by her son Samuel Wiltshire (14), her nephew Robert Rosdale (15), and her brother Lord Frederick Astley (39). HRH Princess Helen, the King's sister, and her husband Charles Astley, the Duke of Arnwall, were unable to attend as they are spending the new year at the Duke's Irish estate, Kirk House. Before lunch, all members of the King and Queen's party attended the Sunday service at St Stephen's Church, with the younger generation braving the cold to walk there and back, greeting the crowds along the route.

In other Fenshire news, the Curson family announced this

morning the unexpected death of Jasmine Curson (32), co-owner of Fenshire-based event's company Posh and Fabulous. In their statement they paid tribute to the high-society 'It' girl, who was dating model Leo Pack, but didn't comment on the cause of Jasmine's death. However Fenshire Police issued a statement saying that a 30 year-old woman was arrested last night in relation to a suspicious death that took place on New Year's Eve at Francis Court. It is believed that Posh and Fabulous were the party planners of the event there. No further information is available at this time.

Meanwhile Lady Beatrice and her business partner Perry Juke, who recently completed phase one of the five-year project to update the interior of Fenn House, will be overseeing the refurbishment of another of the King's private residences, Drew Castle, in Scotland, with work due to start next week.

I hope you enjoyed *Deadly New Year*, If you did then please consider letting others know by writing a review on Amazon or Goodreads, or even both. Thank you.

Will everything go to plan at Drew Castle? Not likely! Look out for the next book in the *A Right Royal Cozy Investigation* series *A Dead Herring*. You can get it from Amazon or wherever you get your paperback books from. **Read chapter 1 on the next page…**

New to the *A Right Royal Cozy Investigation* series? Want to hear more about life (and death) at Francis Court? Find out in *Spruced up for Murder* the first in the A Right Royal Cozy Investigation series available in Amazon or wherever you get your paperback books from. **You can read chapter one on the next but one page.**

For other books in the series take a look at the back of this book.

If you want to find out more about what I'm up to you can find me on Facebook at helengoldenauthor , Instagram at helengolden_author and TikTok at @helengoldenauthor.

Be the first to know when my next book is available. Follow Helen Golden on Amazon, Bookbub, and Goodreads to get alerts whenever I have a new release, preorder, or a discount on any of my books.

CHAPTER 1 — A DEAD HERRING

1:25 pm, Sunday 10 January

Detective Chief Inspector Richard Fitzwilliam wiped his mouth with his napkin and pushed his plate away. "That was just what I needed," he said to the two women sitting opposite him across the wooden dining table that sat along one side of the wall in the living room of the small cottage.

"Thanks for bringing the wood in, Fitz." Emma McKeer-Adler shifted in her seat. "It's normally my job, but…" The petite dark-skinned woman looked down at her right leg, which was stuck out in front of her and slightly to the side, resting on a chair. She grimaced as she studied the heavy white cast covered in scribbles. 'It suits you, ma'am.'; 'Talk about taking one for the team, boss.'; 'My other leg's a mini!'; 'Is it too soon to call you Hop-a-long?'; 'The Cast and the Furious.'; 'Itch here.' She looked back up and shrugged.

"I could have done it," Isobel McKeer-Adler pointed out as she picked up her wineglass and raised it to her lips. "But I always fall over in the snow. I've got no sense of balance. You may have ended up with two broken legs on your plate."

The woman with short blonde hair smiled, her green eyes shining.

"And she'd be an even worse patient than me." Emma patted her wife on the arm. "Wouldn't you, Izzy?"

Izzy grinned and nodded. "As unbelievable as that sounds —" She stopped as Fitzwilliam's mobile phone buzzed and vibrated on the tabletop in front of him.

'Blake' flashed up on the screen, and Fitzwilliam sighed. "Sorry, it's the boss," he told them as he put down his wine-glass and picked up the phone. *He's calling me while I'm on leave; this can't be good.* He hit the call accept button. "Nigel, what can I do for you?"

"Richard, we have a problem at Drew Castle. Are you at Adler's yet?" Superintendent Nigel Blake of the Protection and Investigation (Royal) Service didn't mince words.

Fitzwilliam rubbed his hand across his forehead. "What sort of problem, sir?"

His chest tightened. He knew Lady Beatrice and her business partner were at Drew Castle working on a refurbishment project. Drew Castle was only a mile from the cottage he was staying at while visiting his injured friend and colleague, but he was only planning on being here for a few days. There would be no need to see Lady Beatrice *unless...*

"There's been an unexplained death."

Fitzwilliam's heart skipped a beat. *She's okay, isn't she?*

"Who died?" Fitzwilliam blurted out quickly. Emma raised an eyebrow as she and Izzy leaned across the table, their mouths slightly open.

"A chap called Ben Rhodes. Businessman. He was there as part of a shooting party organised by Lord Frederick Astley."

"Was he shot?"

"No. It looks like he drowned in his bath."

"So it's murder then, sir?"

Adler and Izzy were now so close he could hear their breathing.

"Yes, it seems like it."

Well, of course it will be! Lady Beatrice was a trouble magnet, especially when it came to murder. Fitzwilliam frowned. *But what has this got to do with me? I'm on leave.* He opened his mouth, but his boss got in before he had time to ask.

"The problem is, Richard, they're completely snowed in at Drew Castle. It's unreachable from the outside at the moment. A local lad and the Drew Castle security guys are doing what they can to secure the scene, but I need someone up there overseeing it all and looking out for the family. The Queen Mother is there, along with Lord Frederick, and of course, your *friend*, Lady Beatrice." Could he detect a slight chuckle from his boss? Blake knew full well Lady Beatrice would hardly describe Fitzwilliam as a friend.

"I can't have them up there on their own with a potential murderer running around and no one from PaIRS to keep them safe," Blake continued. "But I can't get anyone to the area until the weather improves. So I think it's serendipitous you're only a short walk away, don't you?"

Serendipitous? Bad luck, more like... Fitzwilliam twisted to look out of the window behind him. It had snowed heavily since he'd been out to collect logs from the wood store behind the cottage, and now a thick blanket of snow smothered everything, leaving only a few outlines of trees looking like large blobs of ice cream. *A short walk?* Not in this weather. He sighed.

"I'm aware you're on leave, Fitzwilliam, and I wouldn't ask if I had any other options." Blake's voice was unexpectedly apologetic.

"Of course, sir. I understand. I'll get there as soon as I can."

"Good-o, Richard. I knew I could count on you. Send my kind regards to Adler, and when this is all over, extend your trip so you still get to spend some additional time there. Detective Sergeant Spicer will be available to you via phone and video, and as soon as the weather gets better, I'll get the local CID over there. Keep me posted."

The line went dead. Fitzwilliam placed his phone back down on the table and rubbed his chin.

"What's happened?" Two pairs of eyes stared across the table at him.

"There's been a murder up at Drew Castle. The boss wants me to take charge. They're snowed in, and no one else can get to them. Although having seen out there" —he gestured towards the window— "I'm not sure I can get there easily either."

Izzy nodded. "You won't be able to drive. The snow's too deep, and it'll be impossible to see where the road is." She got up. "But I think I saw some stuff in the boot room that might be useful."

"Can I come too?" Detective Chief Inspector Emma McKeer-Adler struggled up and gingerly put her weight on her cast.

"No!" Fitzwilliam and her wife cried in unison.

To read more, order your copy of *A Dead Herring* HERE.

CHAPTER 1 — SPRUCED UP FOR MURDER

Early morning, Wednesday 7 April

"Oh my giddy aunt!" Perry Juke slapped his hand up to his mouth, his face turning pale as he gawped at the body in front of them.

"Oh my giddy aunt, indeed," Lady Beatrice, the Countess of Rossex, replied, gazing at the prone form lying only a few metres away from her. Her stomach twisted at the sight of his lifeless body. Instinctively, she wanted to look away, but like a moth attracted to a light, she was drawn to the scene before her.

He — for it was definitely a man with his stocky frame and shaved head — was lying on his front, his arms and legs splayed out, looking rather like he had fallen from a great height. Blood obscured the right-hand side of his face. A patch of what looked like red wine had soaked into the green and black Persian rug underneath his body. The grey marble table, which was normally by the side of the olive-green leather Chesterfield, was lying askew on the floor. One corner was covered in something dark and sticky.

"He must have fallen and hit his head on the table. Is he

dead? He looks very dead," Perry said, scanning the room as if searching for someone to confirm the body was, indeed, dead.

Lady Beatrice raised her hand to her chest to still her racing heart.

The press is going to love this.

A dead body at Francis Court, found by a member of the royal family — this was gold.

She raked her slim fingers through her long auburn hair. If only she hadn't been guilted by her mother into accepting her sister's request to take on the interior design of the refurbished Events Suite, she would be upstairs in her apartment right now, enjoying a leisurely coffee and snuggling with her dog, Daisy. Shaking her head, she returned to the matter in hand. There was possibly a dead body in front of them, and it had to be dealt with.

I suppose one of us needs to check for a pulse.

She turned hopefully to Perry.

To read more, order your copy of *Spruced Up For Murder*

CHARACTERS IN ORDER OF APPEARANCE

DEADLY NEW YEAR

Sophie Crammond — head housekeeper at Francis Court.

Lady Beatrice — The Countess of Rossex. Seventeenth in line to the British throne. Daughter of Charles Astley, the Duke of Arnwall and Her Royal Highness Princess Helen. Niece of the current king.

Perry Juke — Lady Beatrice's business partner and BFF.

Jasmine Curson — co-owner of *Posh and Fabulous* party planners. Sister of Holly.

Charles Astley — Duke of Arnwall. Lady Beatrice's father.

HRH Princess Helen — Duchess of Arnwall. Mother of Lady Beatrice. Sister of the current king.

King James and Queen Olivia — King of England and his wife.

Holly Curson — co-owner of *Posh and Fabulous* party planners. Sister of Jasmine.

Daisy — Lady Beatrice's adorable West Highland Terrier.

Lady Sarah and John Rosdale — Lady Beatrice's elder sister and brother-in-law.

Sam Wiltshire — son of Lady Beatrice and the late James Wiltshire, the Earl of Rossex. Future Earl of Durrland.

Ellie Gunn — Francis Court's catering manager.

Leo Pack — Model. Jasmine Curson's boyfriend.

Aaron Everett — chef for *Posh and Fabulous.*

Robert (Robbie) Rosdale — Lady Sarah's eldest son.

Alex Sterling — the late Francis Court's estate manager.

Mike Ainsley — detective inspector at Fenshire CID.

Simon Lattimore — Perry Juke's partner. Bestselling crime writer. Ex-Fenshire CID. Winner of cooking competition *Celebrity Elitechef.*

Eamon Hines — detective sergeant at Fenshire CID.

Lord Frederick (Fred) Astley — Earl of Tilling. Lady Beatrice's elder brother and twin of Lady Sarah Rosdale. Ex-Intelligence Army Officer. Future Duke of Arnwall.

ALSO BY HELEN GOLDEN

A short prequal in the series A Right Royal Cozy Investigation. Can Perry Juke and Simon Lattimore work together to solve the mystery of the missing clock before the thief disappears? FREE novelette when you sign up to my readers' club. See end of final chapter for details. Ebook only.

First book in the A Right Royal Cozy Investigation series. Amateur sleuth, Lady Beatrice, must pit her wits against Detective Chief Inspector Richard Fitzwilliam to prove her sister innocent of murder. With the help of her clever dog, her flamboyant co-interior designer and his ex-police partner, can she find the killer before him, or will she make a fool of herself?

Second book in the A Right Royal Cozy Investigation series. Amateur sleuth, Lady Beatrice, must once again go up against DCI Fitzwilliam to find a killer. With the help of Daisy, her clever companion, and her two best friends, Perry and Simon, can she catch the culprit before her childhood friend's wedding is ruined?

The third book in the A Right Royal Cozy Investigation series. When DCI Richard Fitzwilliam gets it into his head that Lady Beatrice's new beau Seb is guilty of murder, can the amateur sleuth, along with the help of Daisy, her clever westie, and her best friends Perry and Simon, find the real killer before Fitzwilliam goes ahead and arrests Seb?

A Prequel in the A Right Royal Cozy Investigation series. When Lady Beatrice's husband James Wiltshire dies in a car crash along with the wife of a member of staff, there are questions to be answered. Why haven't the occupants of two cars seen in the accident area come forward? And what is the secret James had been keeping from her?

ALL EBOOKS AVAILABLE IN THE AMAZON STORE.

PAPERBACKS AVAILABLE FROM WHEREVER YOU BUY YOUR BOOKS.

ALSO BY HELEN GOLDEN

When the dead body of the event's planner is found at the staff ball that Lady Beatrice is hosting at Francis Court, the amateur sleuth, with help from her clever dog Daisy and best friend Perry, must catch the killer before the partygoers find out and New Year's Eve is ruined.

Snow descends on Drew Castle in Scotland cutting the castle off and forcing Lady Beatrice along with Daisy her clever dog, and her best friends Perry and Simon to cooperate with boorish DCI Fitzwilliam to catch a killer before they strike again.

A murder at Gollingham Palace sparks a hunt to find the killer. For once, Lady Beatrice is happy to let DCI Richard Fitzwilliam get on with it. But when information comes to light that indicates it could be linked to her husband's car accident fifteen years ago, she is compelled to get involved. Will she finally find out the truth behind James's tragic death?

An unforgettable bachelor weekend for Perry filled with luxury, laughter, and an unexpected death.
Can Bea, Perry, and his hen's catch the killer before the weekend is over?

Bake Off Wars is being filmed on site at Francis Court and everyone is buzzing. But when much-loved pastry chef and judge, Vera Bolt, is found dead on set, can Bea, with the help of her best friend Perry, his husband Simon, and her cute little terrier, Daisy, expose the killer before the show is over?

Printed in Great Britain
by Amazon

39493247R00047